Y0-AEA-259

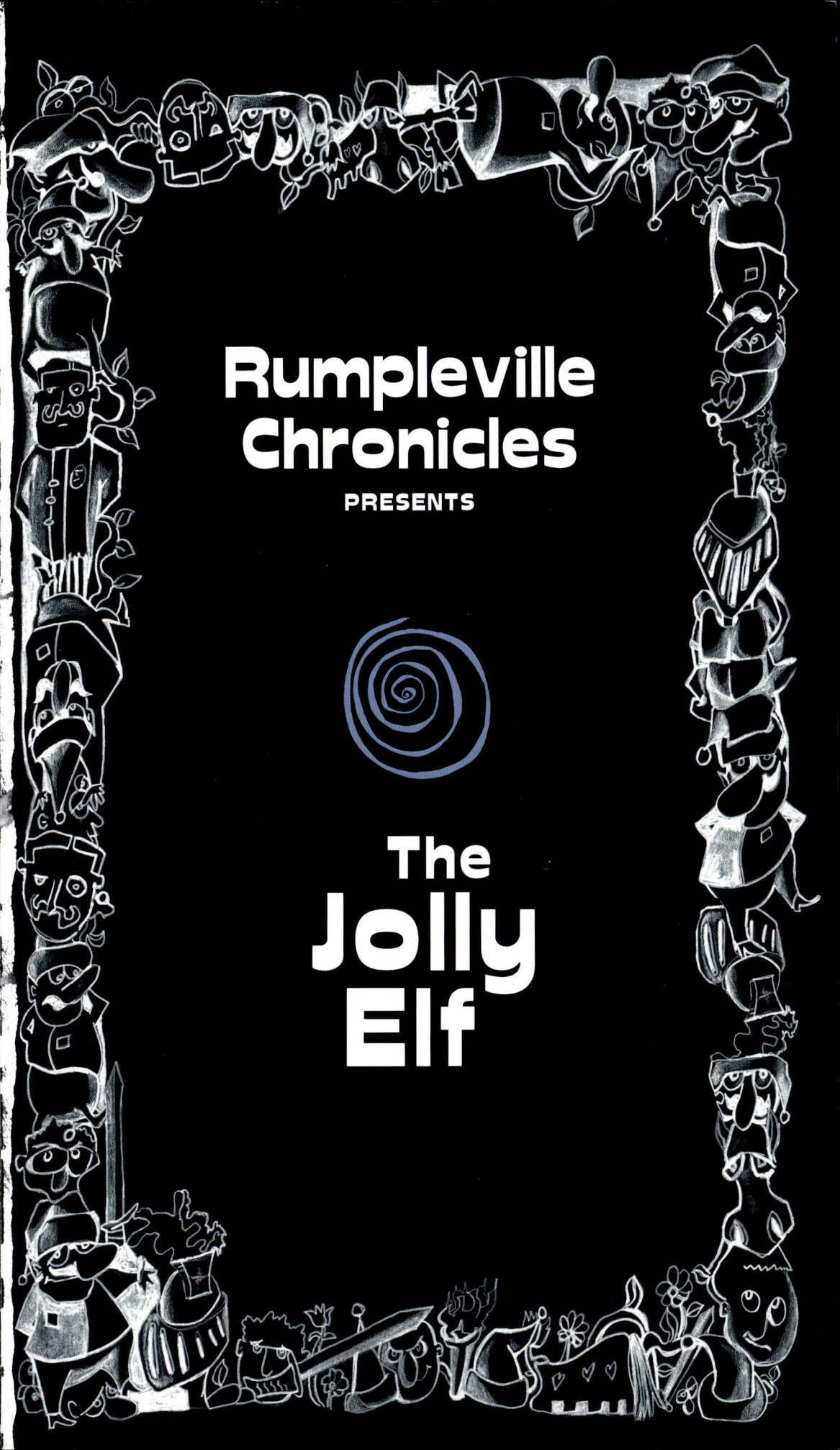

Rumpleville Chronicles

PRESENTS

The Jolly Elf

The Jolly Elf

Written by
Cevin Soling

Illustrated by
Steve Kille

Layout by
Mark Ohe

Production Coordinator
Jim Crotty
Monk Media
www.monkmedia.net

Dedicated to Dr. Claw & Simon
(who sat diligently with Steve while he worked)

SPECTACLE

©2006 Spectacle Films, Inc.
All Rights Reserved

19 West 21st Street #503
New York, NY 10010

Visit our Web Site at
www.rumpleville.com

Library of Congress Control Number: 2006920783
ISBN: 0-9767771-0-X

Printed in China
First Printing February 2006

Deep within the groves of the Coconut Valley...

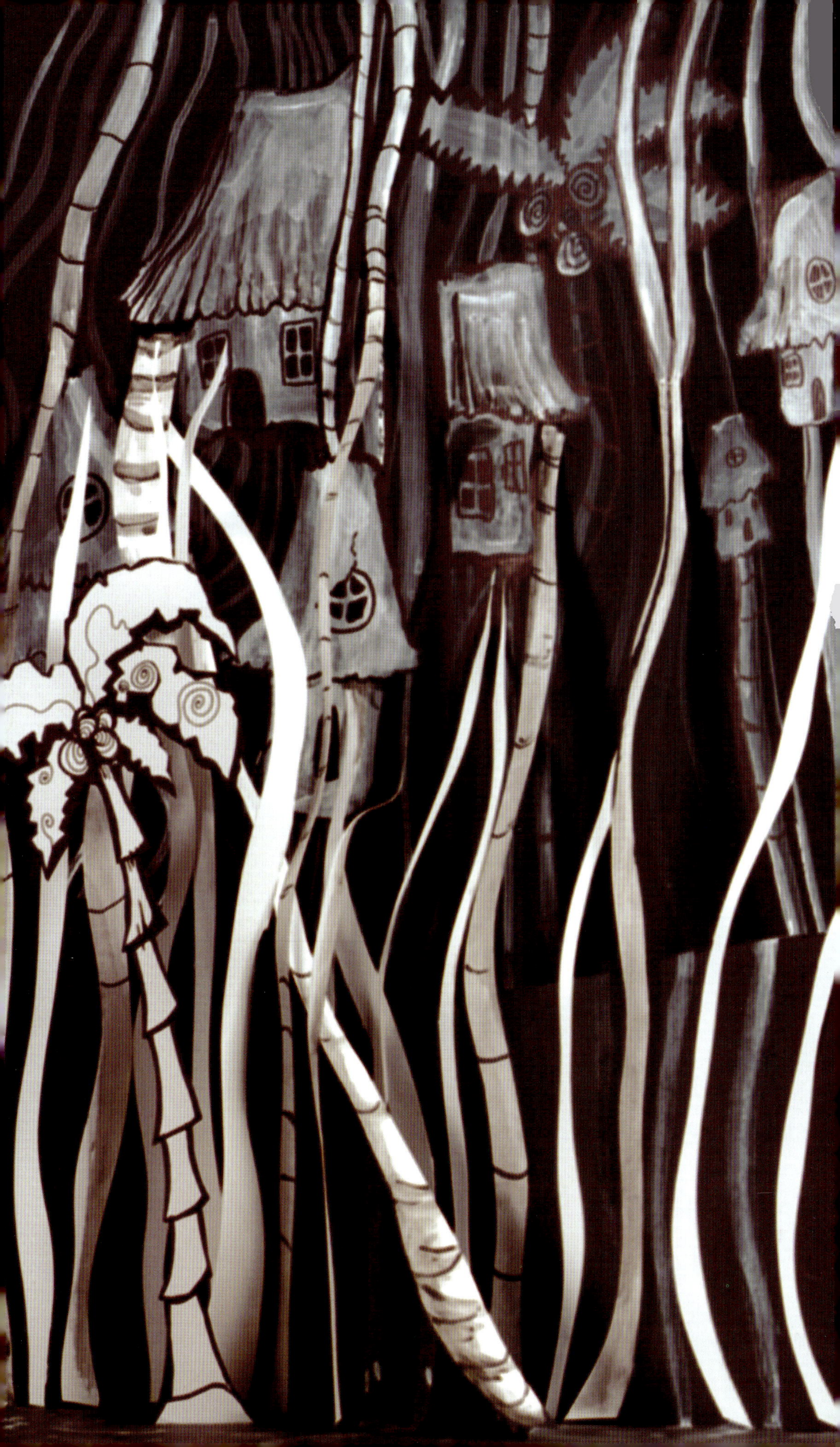

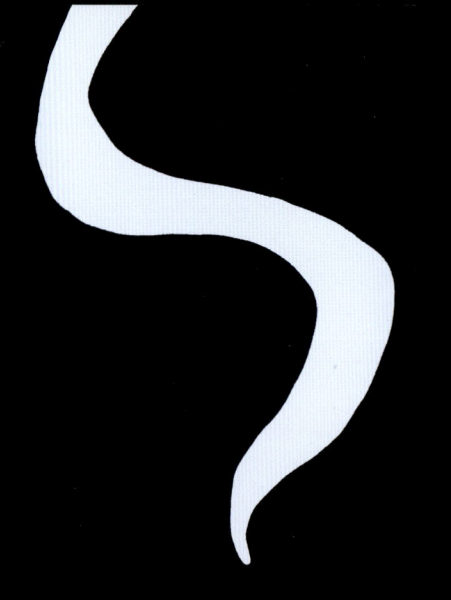

in a remote section of Cuba,

there lived a…

Jolly Elf.

Not only was he jolly,

but he was merry too.

Besides that, he liked to sing.

The Jolly Elf's songs could be heard throughout the entire valley, where he kept local residents up all night long.

Now, in most situations, neighbors complain about noise — especially when it's "Get Up and Boogie" and other disco hits of the Seventies sung at four in the morning.

These residents, however, never complained, except maybe amongst themselves.

And there's a reason too.

It's because the elf was criminally insane and collected shrunken heads. So, the local townsfolk feared him. Whenever they spoke of him, they referred to him as "that psycho jolly merry killer elf who loves to sing (especially at four in the morning)."

The townsfolk knew they had a problem.

So, they went to the yellow pages to see if they could find a knight who

would be willing to destroy the psycho jolly merry killer elf who loves to sing (especially at four in the morning)."

They were unable, however, to find even one knight who would accept the challenge. For while there is great honor to be gained

by slaughtering a ferocious fire-breathing dragon, there is very little for hacking and maiming a midget. So the folk of Coconut Valley were stuck with the psycho jolly merry killer elf who loves to sing (especially at four in the morning). There's a moral in there somewhere.

The Adventures of Waldo

Written by
Cevin Soling

Illustrated by
Steve Kille

Waldo was a chunk of mud. He took a bath and killed himself.

The Jolly Elf

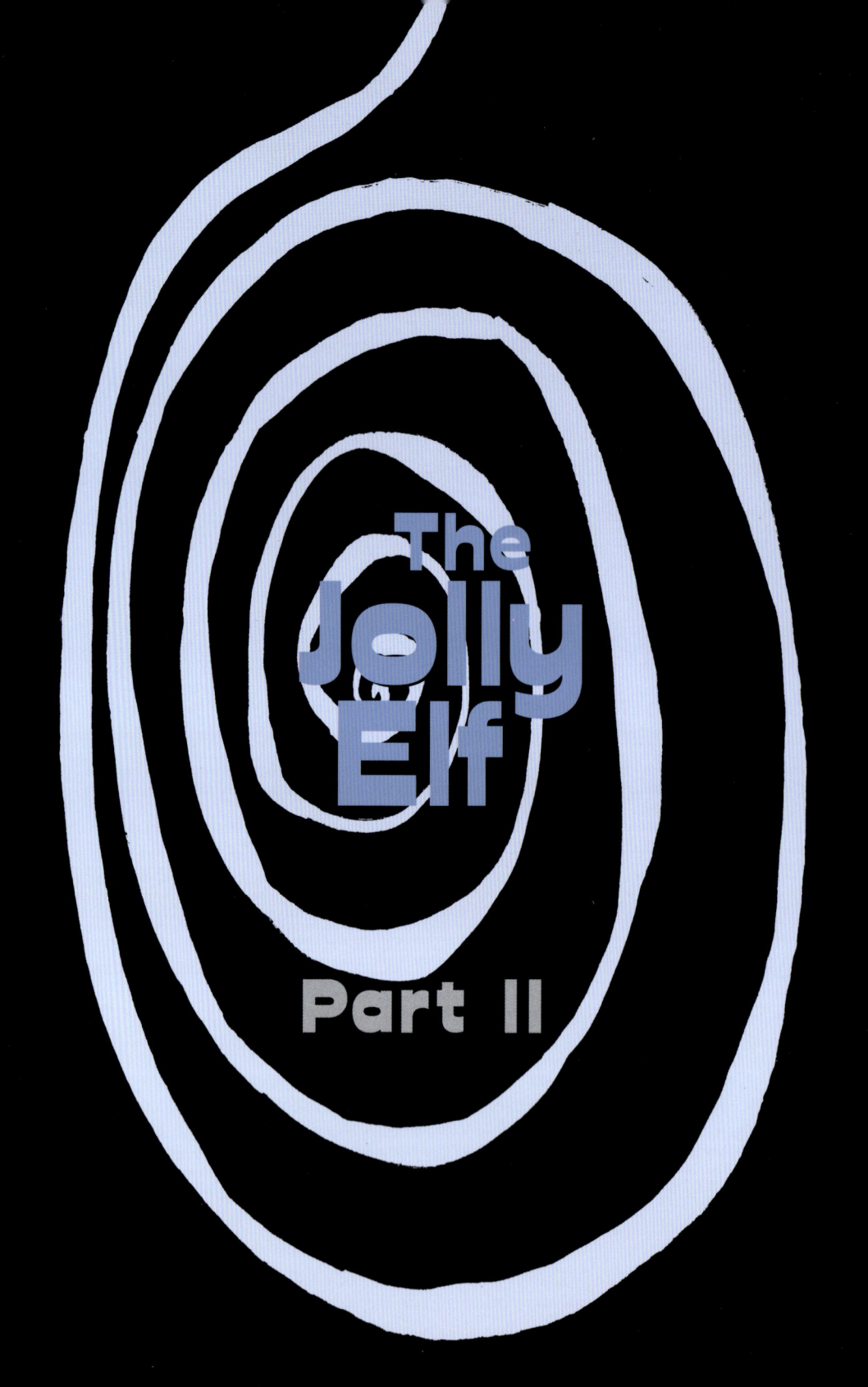

Part II

When the townsfolk that lived deep within the groves of the Coconut Valley in a remote section of Cuba realized that property values were declining due to the psycho jolly merry killer elf who loves to sing (especially at four in the morning), the town was in an uproar.

They quickly organized a lynch mob and went to find the elf.

Their cries for blood echoed throughout the valley, until they reached the ears of the psycho jolly merry killer elf who loves to sing (especially at four in the morning).

Without hesitation, the elf cast a spell that immobilized

all the townsfolk of the Coconut Valley.

Well, almost all the townsfolk.

For some reason his spell did not affect the Mayor of Coconut Valley.

This is because civil servants are used to being in a state of inertia, so immobility would not impede them from performing as they usually do.

When news of the elf's deed spread, there was a bit more interest in the cause. The task of slaying a dwarf did not seem too difficult, but since he was magical, one could still boast.

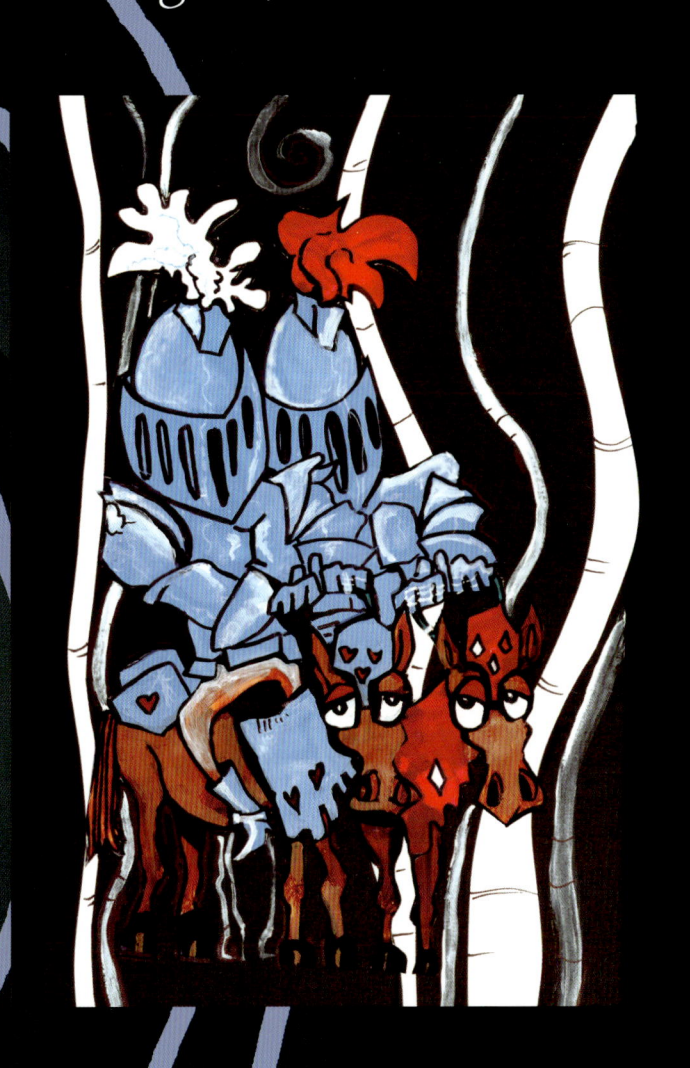

Realizing this, two knights came to the valley to slay the elf: Sir Render and Sir Real. Both were relative unknowns who hoped to gain some publicity.

Before taking on the elf, the knights negotiated with the Mayor of Coconut Valley as to sponsorships, the Cable TV rights to the slaying, and how much the Mayor intended to spend on promotion and advertising.

This plan was counterproductive, as the massive media blitz warned the psycho jolly merry killer elf who loves to sing (especially at four in the morning).

Shortly before the battle was to commence, the elf offered Sir Real some psychedelic mushrooms and a half dozen buttons of peyote if he would end his crusade.

Sir Real agreed to think about it. After ingesting a button or two, he considered the antelopes that were grazing on his skin

and all the
wondrous stars
he inhaled
every time
he breathed.

The pharaohs
smiled at him and
he knew he was one
with all things.

With Sir Real disposed of, Sir Render decided to give up as well. The Mayor took a big loss with the promotional efforts, but hey, it was the

taxpayers' money anyhow, and seeing as they were all paralyzed, his reelection wasn't in jeopardy.

After a couple of days, the elf became quite dejected that his singing bothered no one.

He lifted his spell and freed the people of Coconut Valley …

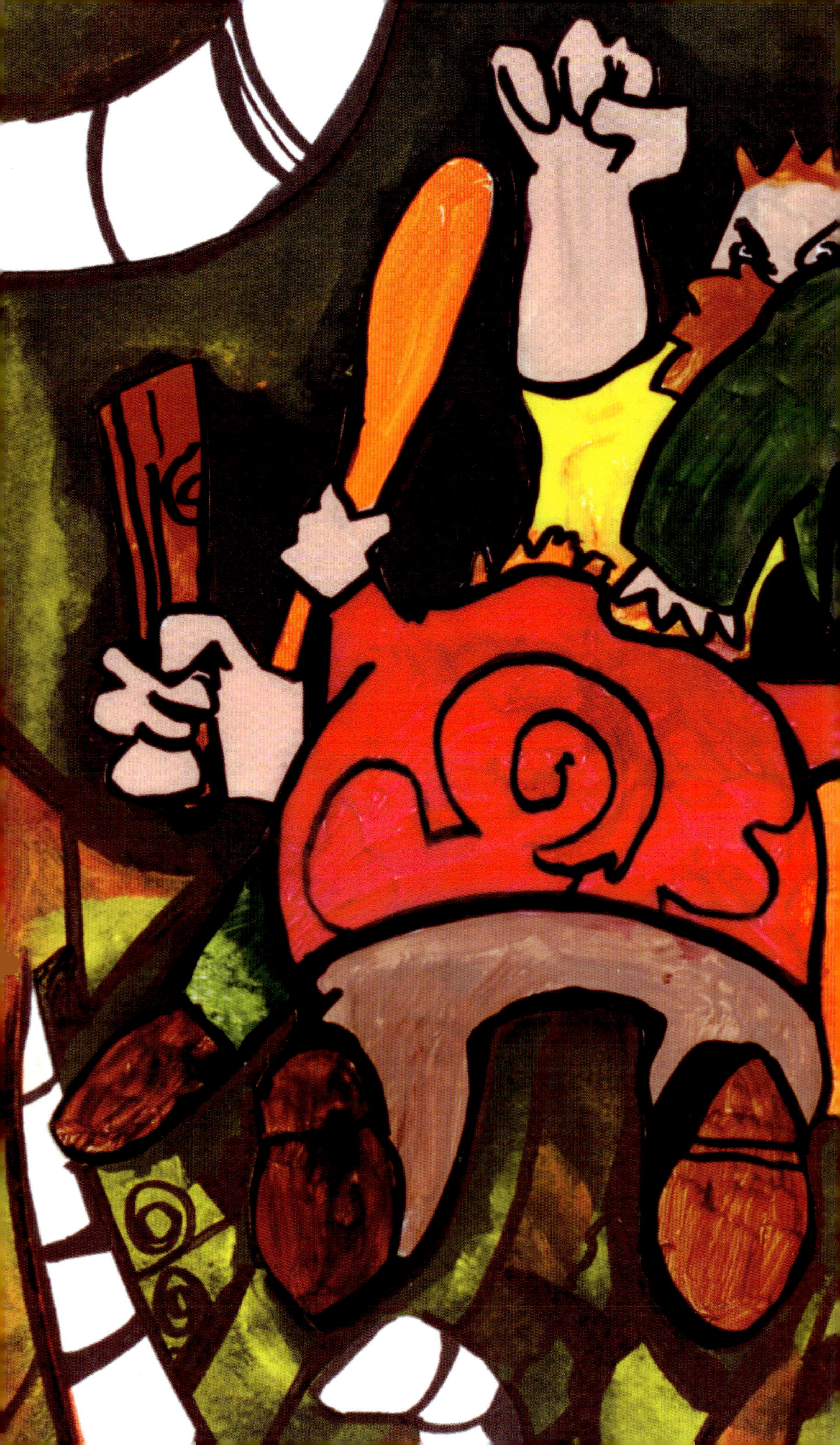

only to be
beaten to death...

and have his head shrunken,

where it eventually found its way
into the Smithsonian Museum.

The End

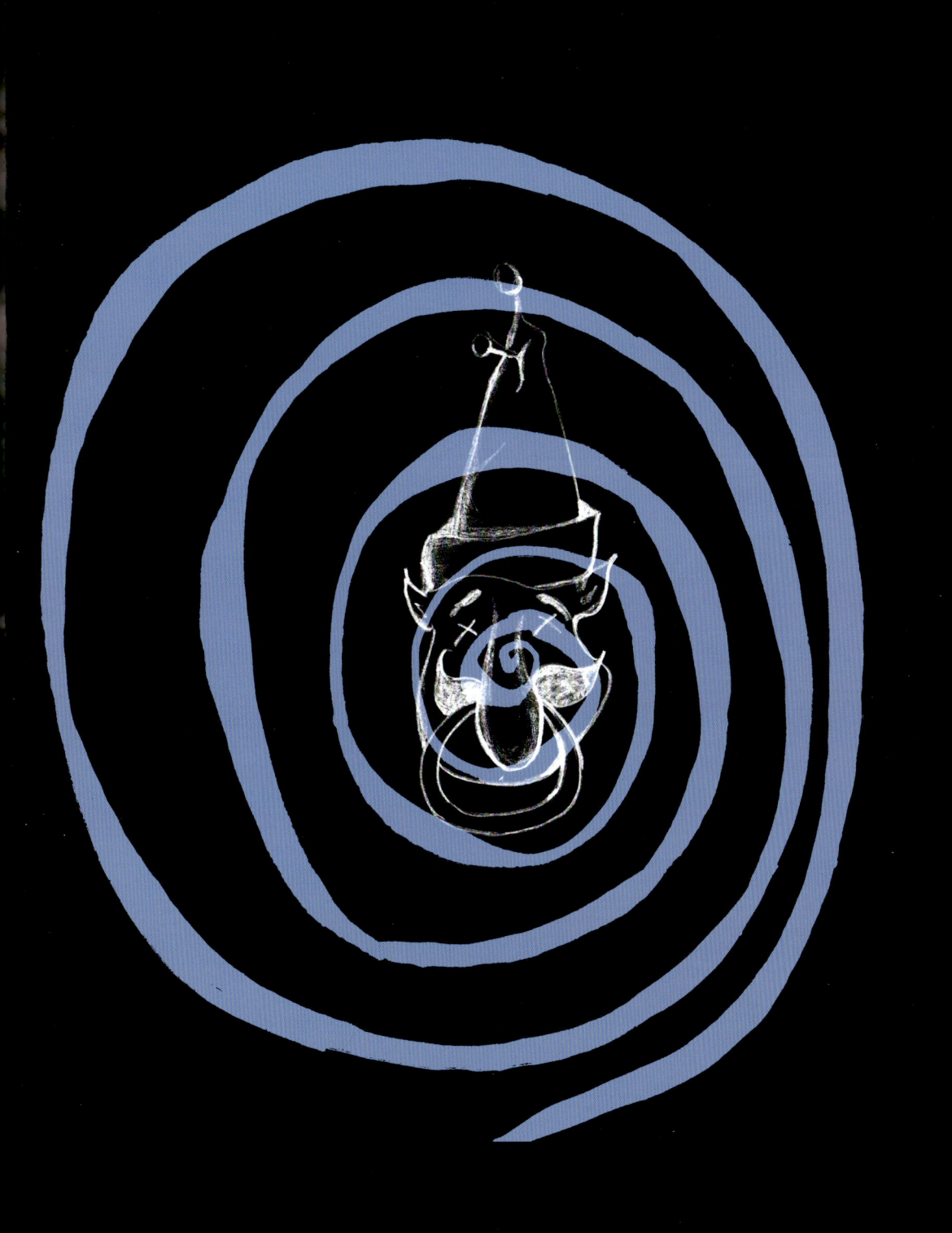